ROBROY

Nº 8

LIBRARY

1ᵈ

ROB ROY TO THE RESCUE

"At that moment a shrill call, clear and cheery, came through the air. It was the war-cry of the MacGregors. Glentive raised his eyes. On the beetling cliff, midway up on a dizzy ledge, stood Rob Roy, waving his bonnet to the astonished MacLeans."

ROB ROY TO THE RESCUE

By ERSKINE BLAIR.

CHAPTER I.

ROB ROY MAKES AN ENEMY.

" LET me but come within striking distance of Rob Roy ! "

It was plain that the laird of Glentive was very angry, and the laird of Glentive was a man whom prudent men sought not to provoke. He was of the Clan Maclean, a giant in stature, with brawny limbs, a broad red face, and a very short temper. His castle, standing on an arm of the sea in the Western Highlands, was an impregnable fortress, and two hundred men able to wield the claymore dwelt upon his estate, and were ready at all times to do his bidding.

Thirty head of cattle had been " lifted " and driven out of Glentive, and the laird had sent word of the theft to Rob Roy, to whom he paid " blackmail " for the protection and recovery of his cattle, and in due time Rob Roy had brought back twenty of the stolen beasts.

But this did not satisfy Glentive, and he had refused to pay Rob Roy any further sums of money whatever ; whereupon Rob Roy had coolly driven off again the cattle he had recovered, under the very nose of the laird, and in spite of the hindrance of the hastily-summoned Macleans.

And so the laird was very wroth, and, with a dozen picked men, had set off in chase of Rob Roy.

" Let me but come within striking distance of the red thief," he blustered, as he hurried through the heather in hot pursuit of the small band of MacGregors who accompanied Rob Roy. " Let me but come nigh him, and I'll whip his head off."

" Eh, but I'm thinking the red chief, or red thief—call him which you will—is a braw hand at sword-play," said the laird's steward, or factor, Duncan Maclean, a shrewd, sly-looking man. " He'll no stand idle, laird, when you come within striking distance."

" And am not I accounted something of a fighter ? " roared the laird. " Dare you tell me that any MacGregor that ever breathed is a match for Maclean of Glentive ? If your heart fails you, Duncan, go home and turn your wife's spinning-wheel, for I'll have no coward loons with me in this business."

" Dinna fash yourself, man," said the factor, with the easy insolence of an old servant, who knows himself to be too valuable to be dismissed for anything he may say or do, " and dinna glower at a body like that. But I'm thinking it's not the MacGregor's head will be lacking if you come to blows."

" You false traitor ! " roared the enraged laird. " Do you tell me to my face that the MacGregor is a better man than I ? "

" Ay, and a better man than all the lords and lairds in Scotland," said Duncan, calmly. " A better man than Argyll, or Athol, or Montrose. You did ill to withhold from him what was justly due, Glentive ; he brought back twenty of the kye, and more he could not do, for the others had been driven by the Macraws further than he could follow them."

" Ay, by his connivance," shouted the laird, furiously.

" I do not think so," said Duncan, coolly. " I trust no man further than

I can help, and of every ten men in Scotland I hold nine to be more canny than honest ; but Rob Roy's an honest man, and never yet went back on his word."

"From this day forth I count him my bitterest foe," said the laird, "and he'll get no more blackmail from me. A thief he is, and to his face I'll tell him so."

"Ay, the opportunity is not lacking," said Duncan, pointing down the glen, where he had sighted some half-dozen red-kilted MacGregors trudging along easily after the slow-going, patient kine that were the cause of this dispute between the mighty laird of Glentive and the chief of the MacGregors.

The sight of those red kilts acted upon the laird as the sight of a red rag is supposed to act upon a bull.

Drawing his tremendous claymore, he called to his men to hasten, and the Macleans, with loud cries, were soon running through the heather after the small band of MacGregors.

The latter turned and, seeing armed men approaching, drew their broadswords—all save one of them, who walked forward a few paces towards the Macleans, and then stood, with arms folded, until the laird was within speaking distance of him.

"How now, Glentive ? " he cried. "What's all this pother about ? "

"Give up my cattle, you red thief," roared the laird, "or not one of you shall ever see Craigrostan again." His clansmen halted about him as he spoke, eager to fall upon Rob Roy's men.

"Pay your dues, laird, and the kye are yours," said Rob Roy.

"Ay, it's with steel I'll pay you," replied the laird.

"We fear not such payment," said Rob Roy, "but it were a pity that brave lads should spill their heart's blood over a parcel of cattle. The dispute is between you and me alone, Glentive. Dare you settle it alone with me ? Dare you cross swords with me, Maclean ? "

"Insolent thief ! " shouted the laird, beside himself with rage. "Not a man of us shall wield his sword but me. Draw, draw, I say."

Rob Roy smiled. His taunt had taken effect. He drew his claymore, and awaited the onrush of the laird, who was a good head taller than himself, and

accounted the strongest man in part of the country.

With a firm wrist Rob Roy held up his sword to guard his head, as the laird of Glentive dealt a lightning-like blow at him.

Again and again the MacGregor warded off the laird's savage blows, while Macleans and MacGregors watched the Titanic combat in breathless silence.

The long swords gleamed in the morning sunshine and clashed together noisily.

The laird hammered at his foe till he was weary, and still Rob Roy stood unharmed behind his sheltering blade, scarcely moving.

Then on a sudden he was all action. Five or six swift blows of steel against steel followed, and the laird's claymore went twirling up into the air over his head, and Rob Roy held the point of his own sword at Maclean's breast.

"I could kill you now, Glentive," he said.

The laird stood straight, without flinching.

"But I will not kill a brave man in cold blood," continued Rob Roy.

The disarmed laird was holding a sprained wrist. He glowered at his opponent in fury.

"You must needs keep to your word," continued Rob Roy ; "your sword and mine were to settle this dispute, and you, at least, will fight no more this day. Farewell to ye, laird of Glentive."

And Rob Roy turned and made a sign to his men to drive on the cattle.

"Ay, I thought Rob Roy would keep his head on his shoulders for aught you might do," said Duncan Maclean, maliciously.

The laird said never a word, but turned and walked back, followed by his crestfallen men.

In his heart he resolved to be avenged upon the man who had held his prowess so lightly. There should be a black feud henceforth between him and the chief of the MacGregors, and he would wait his time and avenge himself upon that insolent Rob Roy.

Now at that time anybody who sought to harm Rob Roy had the law of Scotland on his side, for the MacGregor was an outlaw, and anyone might apprehend him and hand him over to justice who could.

Maclean did not forget this fact ; and would it not be a fine revenge, he thought, to have Rob Roy captured and sent, bound hand and foot, to Edinburgh?

The laird of Glentive thought much upon this matter during the next few days.

CHAPTER II. •

THE CROSS-EYED MAN.

There was a guest at the castle of Glentive, a guest who seemed in high favour with the laird, but whose presence was very odious to Effie Maclean, the laird's only daughter. This was Roger Fargus, a man of about forty years of age, who ordinarily lived in Glasgow. Fargus was half Scotch, half English; his face was marked with small-pox, the scourge of that age, and his small eyes seemed intent upon trying to look into one another, for he was afflicted with a terrible squint.

But it was not merely his appearance that made him odious in Effie's eyes. If common report was true, there was blood on his hands. He had been once tried for murder, in Glasgow, but the lawyers who defended him had got him off with a verdict of "not proven."

He was also reported to make a good living by bearing false witness in the law courts. After the Jacobite rising he was believed to have sworn away the lives of many innocent men who were obnoxious to the Whig lords who secretly employed him.

No work was too dirty for Roger Fargus, so long as it was paid for; and it was this man of evil repute whom Maclean of Glentive now entertained at his table; and Effie wondered that her father, who was a proud man, should ask such a guest to break bread with him. But her father had been strangely morose of late.

When Fargus had been three days in the house Effie plucked up courage to remonstrate with her father.

"I heartily wish, father," she said, "you would send that odious man about his business. Why comes he here?"

The laird, who was a widower, had but one soft spot in his heart, and that was for his only child; but upon this occasion he answered her rather harshly.

"Go to your spinning or your books, girl," he said, "and meddle not with my affairs."

"But, father, they say such evil things of Fargus."

"They say? Who say? Fargus is my good friend. But 'tis ever the way of women to judge a man by his looks. Well, if a handsome young gallant is more to your liking we shall have one here anon, for Sir James Oldcastle from Northumberland is to be my guest presently. His eyes look out straight beneath his brows, I promise you. Will that satisfy you? Now go about your business, and bear with an ugly man's company for awhile, and you shall not lack good-looking company later."

"Handsome or ill-favoured, 'tis all one to me," replied Effie, with lofty indifference, "but I would that our guests were gently born and gentle-mannered."

"Why, what discourtesy has Fargus showed ye?" demanded her father.

"He has showed me none, but——"

"But the small-pox has scarred him, and so he is a villain! Away, lass; I have no more patience with ye," said the laird, roughly, as he turned on his heel. And Effie went to her own rooms, angered at having being misjudged. What cared she, indeed, for a man's looks!

In the meanwhile the laird was closeted in a room leading off the hall with the object of Effie's aversion. Perhaps, had she seen him at that moment, her heart would have lightened somewhat, for Fargus had got into a pair of jackboots, and held his hat in one hand and his riding-whip in the other. He was evidently bound upon a journey, and was taking a last glass of wine with the laird before setting out.

"You are sure you are taking enough men with you?" said the laird.

Fargus smiled, with both eyes staring at the tip of his nose as it seemed.

"Three stout fellows will do the business, laird, with me to think for them," he replied.

"Good. And remember, my hand must appear nowhere in this, or Glentive will be raided for ever after by the rascally MacGregors."

"It shall all appear," said Fargus, "as if the business had its inception in Glasgow. Why, what more natural than that the Courts should send out their minions to take an outlaw?"

"True," said the laird, "true."

"Your men have doffed their tartans."

"Ay, they look for all the world like poor Lowland caitiffs."

Fargus grinned.

"There is one danger, though," said the laird; "when their blood is hot they may raise the slogan of the clan, and so betray themselves and me."

"I will see to it that they do not," said Fargus.

"You are very confident you can manage this affair."

"Confident? Pshaw! I wish I often had a chance of earning Scotch gold so easily. I shall do it as easily as I empty this glass."

As the sinister-looking fellow had certainly experienced no difficulty in performing the latter feat three or four times in quick succession, the laird might perhaps have been expected to have felt reassured.

But his face was still troubled when he took leave of Fargus. Perhaps he had not yet wholly conquered his pride, and felt that he had committed himself to a very ignoble and crooked line of conduct. Perhaps Effie's words had caused him some twinges of conscience. At all events, his temper did not amend after Fargus had ridden away in the darkness, accompanied by three strapping Mac-Leans, in the unaccustomed livery of riding coats and breeches, and Effie wondered what had come over her father, and why he was so gloomy and morose.

After leaving Glentive Castle, which he did about nine o'clock on a spring evening, Fargus rode steadily forward for some hours. He was a talkative, humorous fellow, or he could be so when he pleased, and upon this occasion he kept his companions entertained with his tales of the life—strange to them—of great cities, such as Glasgow, Edinburgh, and London. He was very anxious to keep the men in good humour, the more so because he was shrewd enough to understand that, although they were employed upon the all-powerful laird's business, the work in hand was not much to their liking.

The four men rode all night; by daybreak they were near Rob Roy's home at Craigrostan, and Fargus, having ordered his men to tether their horses at a little distance from the roadside, and to await his return, and having given them certain other instructions, rode on alone to the house which Rob Roy then occupied.

He found the chief standing outside the door of his house, having just risen.

Fargus doffed his hat.

"Good-day to you, sir," he said.

"Good-day to you," replied Rob Roy.

"I have the honour, I believe, of addressing Robert MacGregor, otherwise called Rob Roy," continued Fargus.

"If you esteem it an honour, sir," said Rob Roy.

"The friend of the poor, the righter of wrongs," said Fargus. "I come to ask a service of you, Rob Roy," he added.

"How may I serve you?" asked the chief.

"Oh, 'tis not for myself that I ask your help," said Fargus, "but for a poor, timorous body, a Campbell, whose cows have been lifted. He is a poor man, sir, and the loss of his cows means ruin to him. It was the MacRaws that played him this trick."

"And why comes he not in person to ask my help?" demanded Rob Roy.

"Because," said Fargus, "he is, as I have said, a poor frightened body, and some months ago he was so unfortunate as to quarrel with one of your men, and, as I understand, to wound him. For this reason he is afraid to show himself here, fearing his enemy may be about the place. I must tell you the quarrel was none of his seeking, but when I advised him to seek your help against the MacRaws, he said he doubted you would aid one who had quarrelled with one of your clansmen. 'Pshaw! man,' said I, 'Rob Roy is reported to have a generous heart, and to be a friend of the poor. Moreover, he is a foe to these thieving MacRaws.'"

"That is true," said Rob Roy; "but you seem very earnest on his behalf."

"The man has done me some service," said Fargus. "After the late rising he sheltered me in his house while King George's redcoats were hunting for me. I owe him some return, therefore. But, indeed, the service I do him is little enough. I was travelling this way, in any case, so I offered to intercede with you for him, and truly I hope you will get back the poor man's cattle."

"It shall be done," said Rob Roy; "but whither have the MacRaws driven them?"

"Nay, you must ask him that," said Fargus. "I am, as you see, an Englishman, and know not the names of your straths and glens, your hills and your horrible wildernesses. Campbell himself will tell you which way they have gone."

"Very well," said Rob Roy, "you may tell your friend he can come here in safety, and none of my clansmen shall harm him."

"He is hiding in the glen below," said Fargus, "not half a mile from here," and he pointed with his riding-whip down the hillside.

"Oh ! he is a foolish body if he will not venture here," said Rob Roy.

"So I told him myself," agreed Fargus.

"Go ! tell him to come. But stay, you have travelled far and are in need of refreshment. Come into my house. We will break our fast, and afterwards I will accompany you and have speech with your friend."

Fargus, unseen by the chief, grinned with complacency. His plot was succeeding.

He had no scruple whatever about accepting the hospitality of the man he was going to betray, and followed him into his house, where he was well entertained.

After breakfast Rob Roy, unarmed save for a dirk, accompanied Fargus, who went on foot leading his horse. They descended the hill, and when they were about half a mile from Rob Roy's house Fargus began to call upon the imaginary Campbell to show himself.

"The foolish fellow must have taken fright at the sight of some of your men," said Fargus, "and strayed back along the valley."

Still suspecting no harm, Roy Roy accompanied the cross-eyed man until his house was nearly a mile behind him.

"Campbell ! man Campbell ! " cried Fargus again.

This was the signal to his followers. The three sturdy MacLeans sprang out from among some bushes, and at the same moment Fargus sprang like a tiger-cat upon Rob Roy, who was so taken by surprise that he had not time to draw his dirk.

He flung Fargus from him, however, but only to find himself the next instant in the grasp of the three MacLeans.

They were all powerful men, chosen for their great strength, and Rob Roy was no more than human. After a desperate struggle the great chief was bound. Even then he raised his voice and cried for help. But he gave only

one cry, for he was promptly gagged. Then he was hoisted on to a horse, behind one of the MacLeans, and the whole party set off briskly in order to get away from the MacGregors' country as speedily as might be.

"It's to Glasgow town we're taking you," said Fargus. "You have set the law at defiance long enough, and you must know I represent the law."

So the cross-eyed man shielded the laird of Glentive from the reproach of having brought about this capture.

CHAPTER III.
A DARING ESCAPE.

Rob Roy blamed himself bitterly for his easy credulity that had led him to believe Fargus's tale so readily. It was some small satisfaction to know that the treacherous cross-eyed man had not come off scot-free in the recent tussle ; for the chief could see that he was bleeding from a scalp wound, his head having come into contact with a stone when he was flung down.

But this was all the satisfaction Rob Roy could derive from his present unhappy situation.

All day he was borne along at a rapid rate over the hills, and not once did he sight the tartan of a clansman who might spy his luckless condition and summon the MacGregors to his aid.

After the midday halt for rest and refreshment Rob Roy was ungagged, and his bonds were arranged more easily. He was, in fact, merely bound to the man behind whom he rode by a broad leather strap, which passed round both of them. This left his hands free.

But still, escape seemed impossible, or the bonds would have been doubled in strength. Behind the captive rode Fargus with a loaded pistol in his hand. On either side of the captive rode the laird's men, each likewise armed with pistols, "which," as Fargus said, "will go off if you show the least disposition to escape."

"If these are Glasgow men," thought Rob Roy, "they show a strange knowledge of the country, for they have kept out of sight of all the places where there might be men who would help me."

But there was no doubt about the fact that they were certainly making for Glasgow.

Nothing could be more terrible to the

chief than the prospect of imprisonment. Accustomed to live as free as air, amidst mountains and lakes, he would be like an eagle in a cage.

For some time the idea had been growing upon him that he knew the face of the man to whom he was bound.

" He, at least, is no Glasgow body," he thought.

Then he thought of his recent quarrel with MacLean of Glentive, and decided that this man must be a MacLean. So, when the dusk had come upon them, he whispered :—

" Man MacLean ! "

The man in front of him turned his head sharply.

Rob Roy laughed. " Ay, I knew you for one of Glentive's men," he said, now convinced of the correctness of his guess.

The man mumbled something indistinctly.

" MacLean," said Rob Roy, " this is dirty work for a brave Highland laddie. When the mirk comes, you'll loose the buckle of this bonny braw strap that makes us closer than brothers, and I'll be skipping. This is no work for a brave laddie."

" 'Twould be worse work for a brave laddie," said the man, " to get a bullet in my back from that squint-eyed rascal behind me."

" Oh ! the squint-eyed man cannot shoot straight."

" Ay, he can ! " said the man.

" They'll hang me up in Glasgow," continued Rob Roy.

" 'Tis not my fault if they do," replied the man.

Ultimately Rob Roy saw he was to expect no help from this man, who, without being hostile, had more regard for his own skin than for Rob Roy's safety.

The dark came on apace, and suddenly a rapturous thought flashed into Rob Roy's mind.

Thenceforward his gloom left him.

They rode on till they reached the brink of a wide river.

One of the men led the way to a ford.

Before the horses took to the water, Fargus came up to Rob Roy and examined his bonds.

" Oh ! they'll hold," said Rob Roy, carelessly.

" I'll warrant they will," rejoined Fargus, with a wicked laugh. " Ay,

and if they did chance to slip in mid-stream I shall be close behind you, Rob Roy, to give you a hand if you get into deep water."

" I'm obliged to ye," said the chief. " And I think the water is truly deep to-night."

The river was indeed swollen, as Rob Roy had said. The first horse was already in water up to its girths, but the ford was practicable with care.

The horse upon which Rob Roy was mounted soon stepped into the river and reached mid-stream. Fargus's horse refused the water at first, and the space between Rob Roy and Fargus was, for a few seconds, considerable.

The MacGregor made good use of those few seconds. Raising his knee, he snatched from his stocking a small dirk, which his captors had not thought to take from him. It was the recollection that this was still in his possession which had brought such joy to the captive's heart a little while before.

While the horse floundered in deep water, which was swishing about the rider's ankles, Rob Roy with one dexterous cut severed the leather strap that bound him and his fellow-rider together.

The next moment he had slipped into the water. Instantly there was uproar and commotion. Fargus plunged wildly forward through the water and fired his pistol.

The man to whom Rob Roy had been bound, foreseeing trouble to himself if the MacGregor got away, fired also.

But Rob Roy had dived under the water and was swimming down stream. He rose, and saw two of the men galloping in the darkness along the bank, ready to fire at him.

Under he went again, leaving his plaid floating on the surface.

Shot after shot was fired at this, until the men discovered what it was. By that time Rob Roy was some distance from his late captors.

Before morning he was safely at home again, inditing a reproachful letter to the laird of Glentive.

" Though it is honourable for one gentleman to encounter another with the sword," he wrote, " yet there are tools which a man may not with credit employ, and if you send another messenger like the last, I will send him back to Glentive with his ears cropped."

Upon receiving this letter the laird of Glentive was thrown into such a towering passion that even Effie was frightened of him.

But the worst of the laird's anger was for Fargus, and not for Rob Roy.

"The villain has betrayed me as well as failed me," he said ; and it was well for Fargus that he kept out of the way.

The laird thought that his cattle would suffer after this exploit, and he thought rightly. The horned population of Glentive decreased rapidly during the next few weeks, until the MacGregors considered that they had exacted a sufficient fine for the indignity which had been put upon their chief.

So the feud between Rob Roy and the laird of Glentive increased in bitterness, and Glentive vowed to be quits with his enemy yet.

CHAPTER IV.

Showing the Perils of Boastfulness.

"You think, my lord Duke, the man is to be relied on ? "

"Ay, he is a desperate rascal, a broken gambler ; when a man has naught to lose and much to gain he is likely to be bold."

The laird of Glentive and the Duke of Montrose were seated together in a gloomy, lofty apartment in a house in Edinburgh.

MacLean, plotting afresh against Rob Roy, had sought an audience of Rob Roy's great enemy, the Duke of Montrose, and the upshot of their meeting was that a reward had been publicly offered to any man who would evict the outlawed MacGregor.

The bait had tempted a daring, dissolute young man, named Moncrieff, who, as the Duke had said, had squandered a fortune in play, and was eager to repair his broken luck.

"The red thief has long been a thorn in my side, my lord Duke," said MacLean.

"Ay, he shall trouble you no more, nor me either," replied the Duke, "when once I have a tractable tenant at Balquidder in his place. Moreover, Moncrieff avers he will carry Rob Roy in custody to Stirling."

A smile of satisfaction illumined the laird's broad face.

"If he can do that," he said, "I will add a hundred guineas to his reward. But I would not have my name appear anywhere in this business, or the MacGregors will be raiding my cattle again. But if Moncrieff can do this, he is indeed a valiant man."

"You shall judge of him for yourself," said the Duke. "I never saw so desperate a rogue."

Shorty after this, Moncrieff, for whom they had been waiting, entered the room, announced by a servant.

He advanced, with insolent nonchalance, towards the top of the room, where the Duke and his ally were sitting.

"He is a greater rascal than Fargus," thought the laird, as he watched the young man approach, and noted his daring, insolent look, his bold eyes, his shabby clothes stained with wine, and his hungry appearance.

"Ruined, starving, reckless," meditated MacLean; "of good blood, which ensures courage—yes, he is like to prove a dangerous man to the red chief."

Moncrieff bowed with careless ceremony.

"So," said the Duke, "you are still determined to undertake this business."

"Ay, my lord," replied Moncrieff, idly tapping his fingers on his sword hilt. "Dice and cards have played me false. I'm ready for fresh diversion."

"You will, of course, take sufficient force with you to assure success. Rob Roy has many friends," continued Montrose.

"I have chosen six picked men, my lord."

"Only six ! "

"It will suffice. Six villainous rascals, I assure you, my lord, who would cut your throat for sixpence, or this gentleman's either."

Neither the Duke nor the laird seemed to care for this guarantee of character.

"Well, well," said Montrose, "doubtless you know best how to choose your tools. When do you start ? "

"Oh, at once, my lord—to-night. I am itching to touch that gold."

"And you will endeavour to bring Rob Roy in custody to Stirling ? "

"Endeavour ? I will do it."

"I will add a hundred guineas to your reward if you do so," put in MacLean, eagerly.

Moncrieff turned his insolent gaze upon the laird, and looked him up and down.

"I thank ye," he said, coolly. Then

he laughed. "Gadzooks, if I had your inches I would not bribe any man to take my enemies for me."

"There are some things," said Mac-Lean, with dignity, "that a gentleman cannot very well do, and MacLean of Glentive is not likely to turn sheriff's officer."

Moncrieff flushed darkly, and his brows contracted. Then his careless air returned to him.

"As to that," he said, "let me tell you that Moncrieff, of nowhere in particular, has as good blood in his veins as MacLean of Glentive, and Moncrieff, of nowhere, is willing to risk his skin while MacLean of Glentive twiddles his thumbs at home, and lets other men do his dirty work. I don't know which gives better proof of his gentility, do you, my lord?" he asked of the Duke, with a cynical laugh.

The laird frowned, the Duke frowned, and Moncrieff, fearing he might lose the promised reward if he continued in this strain, changed the subject, and asked the Duke if he had any particular instructions to give him.

"I think," replied Montrose, "you are in no need of tutoring where a desperate venture is concerned. Remember that it is a desperate venture. Rob Roy is fierce as an eagle and elusive as a fox. My own men have failed against him more than once."

"Your Grace is unfortunate in your servants," replied Moncrieff, bowing low, and then quitting the room with a jaunty air.

That night he set out with his six men for the MacGregors' country.

The seven travellers arrived in due time at an inn very near to Rob Roy's farm, and entered it to refresh themselves, without knowing that its landlord was a MacGregor.

The whisky was good, and loosened the travellers' tongues, and Moncrieff began to speak boastfully to the landlord of the house, who seemed a simple sort of fellow.

"You see my six rascals," he said, pointing to his followers; "I warrant they're a match for any men in these parts. I have heard much of the wild MacGregors, but I can assure you I fear them not."

"The MacGregors will not harm peaceable travellers," replied the landlord, "such as I take you to be."

"Oh! ay! we're peaceable enough," replied Moncrieff; "we're law-abiding folk. In fact, we're on our way to execute the law upon a noted freebooter."

"Say you so—a freebooter?"

"Yes; and an outlaw. And I think we are not far from his hiding-place. Perhaps you can direct us to Rob Roy's farm."

"I can do that," said the landlord; "it is not half a mile from here. But, if you have told me the truth about your errand, I shall but be directing you to your death. Rob Roy will be taken by no man. Turn back, young man, and save your skin."

Moncrieff laughed, and faced the landlord.

"Look you, my friend," he said; "look at me well. I have fought more duels than you have fingers on your hands. My villains here have more blood on their hands than they have whisky in their stomachs, and that is saying a good deal. Do you think we are to run from your bare-legged fire-eater? Tush! man, send a boy along with me to guide me on my way, and it shall be a guinea in your pocket. I will go first alone to see Rob Roy, in the guise of a benighted traveller, lest he should take fright from seeing seven men at once, and so attempt to escape."

"If you will not be persuaded," said the landlord, "I will send my boy with you. I will go and seek him."

"Do so," laughed Moncrieff.

The landlord went out of the room, and despatched his ostler hastily to warn Rob Roy that there were enemies at hand. Then he returned to Moncrieff with his son, who was to guide the party to Rob Roy's house.

After another glass round of good Scotch spirits the seven desperadoes left the inn, and followed their guide until they were in sight of Rob Roy's farm.

Moncrieff dismissed the boy, and hid his six men in a coppice hard by the house.

"Now, you rascals," he said, "come when I whistle to ye, and the bird is caught; and thank your stars that I have put you in the way of earning money so easily."

Then, with a jaunty tread, he walked to Rob Roy's door and rapped upon it with his knuckles.

The chief in person responded to the summons.

"Who's there?" he asked.

"Sir," said Moncrieff, "I've lost my way amongst these wild mountains, and I make bold to ask you if you will afford me shelter, or, at least, put me into the right road for Glasgow."

"Come in," said Rob Roy, heartily; "no hungry man shall ever be denied a place at my board while I have aught to set before him. Come in."

"That I will," replied Moncrieff, "for the mountain air has sharpened my hunger."

In a few minutes he was sitting at table with the chief and his wife and one of his sons.

Rob Roy talked with his guest in the friendliest manner during supper, and the rascally fellow laughed inwardly to think what an easy prey the noted chief would be.

"He is a mild fellow," he thought, "a soft, simple fellow, and it is plain that he ill deserves the reputation men give him for boldness."

Certainly Rob Roy talked as if he was nothing but a peaceable farmer, and Moncrieff was certain of the success of his undertaking when, at the end of supper, the chief invited him into another apartment.

"Where," he said, "we will brew a bowl of punch, and you shall tell me how the world wags in Edinburgh. For we are simple folks here, and do not often have a chance of a crack with any one from the city. Follow me, sir."

"This could not be bettered," thought Moncrieff, following the chief into another room, where a rushlight was burning, dimly illumining the chamber.

He had but just stepped over the threshold when he came to a halt.

"Come in," said Rob Roy.

But Moncrieff stood as if turned to stone. He was ordinarily a bold fellow, but much dissipation had played tricks with his nerves, and, indeed, the sight that met his gaze was enough to shake a brave man.

Suspended from the rafters a man was hanging by the neck, the body gently swaying in the draught from the open door.

"What's that?" he whispered.

"That?" rejoined Rob Roy. "Oh! that is the body of an impudent dog of a messenger who came to serve a summons upon me yesterday. I thought he had been cut down ere now, but I suppose my men have been too busy to think on it."

Moncrieff still stood staring at the hanging body. What sort of a house was this into which he had come? All the while that its inmates had been sitting at supper this body had been hanging in the next room. There seemed to be a degree of cold-blooded callousness about these MacGregors that was shocking even to Moncrieff, who now saw that his task was not likely to be an easy one.

His task was, in point of fact, never to be accomplished.

Before he had recovered from his surprise Rob Roy shouted aloud, and half-a-dozen clansmen dashed into the room and seized Moncrieff, who expected nothing less than to be strung up beside the murdered messenger. But the MacGregors were more merciful than that. They contented themselves with carrying Moncrieff out and throwing him into the icy river hard by.

His men saw what had happened, and fled in a panic. But kilted MacGregors sprang up from the ground all about them, and the most active of them all was the landlord of the inn. The six ruffians were all overpowered, borne struggling to the river, and ducked again and again, until they were half-drowned. Then they were suffered to crawl away amidst the jeers of the MacGregors; and Rob Roy returned home, and cut down the dummy figure that he had hanged from his rafters.

"I think," he said to his wife, "that for this kindness I am indebted to MacLean of Glentive. Aweel! to-morrow my lads shall drive his kye once more, to teach him better manners."

And Moncrieff, morose and ashamed, was trudging homewards, wishing that he had not been so boastful at the inn.

CHAPTER V.

THE PEDLAR.

Once more MacLean of Glentive suffered the pangs of disappointment and rage, and the loss of his cattle.

In a frenzy of rage he sent a letter to Rob Roy, telling him that if ever he dared to venture near Glentive again he should be shot like a fox, for in that.

part of the country vulpecide was not esteemed a crime.

To this harmless threat Rob Roy returned an insolent answer. "I shall come and go in Glentive," he wrote, "without asking leave of the laird."

MacLean read this letter, and told himself he would bide his time; open warfare was not convenient just now, for he had guests at the castle—two English knights from the North country, whom he did not wish to shock by a display of Highland savagery.

These two guests were both young and rich, and their names were Sir James Oldcastle and Sir Ralph Couldrey. The canny Scots laird had hopes of seeing his daughter Effie united to one of them, for they were richer men than any of the neighbours who were likely to sue for her hand.

Sir James Oldcastle was a dark, handsome man, tall, bold, and of uncertain temper. Sir Ralph, who was the younger of the two, was fair, and possessed of great amiability of manner.

Whatever the laird's hopes or plans might have been, it was plain that Effie, who was only seventeen years of age, regarded the young men merely as guests and friends. She accepted their compliments with a gracious dignity, she met their looks of admiration with perfect unconsciousness; and neither young man had any reason to flatter himself that he could win the laird's daughter. But Sir James Oldcastle vowed to himself that Effie MacLean should be his wife.

There had been a great hunting of the deer, and at the close of the day MacLean's household assembled in the great hall of the castle to banquet.

Towards the end of the meal there was some disturbance outside the door of the hall, and the laird asked one of the servants what it meant.

"'Tis an old pedlar, sir," replied the man, "who seeks entrance to the hall. He has been selling his wares to the maids in the kitchen, and now would approach your worship, but I have told him the thing is not to be thought of."

"Why, let him come in if he will," said the laird, good-humouredly. "What say you, Sir Ralph?"

"With all my heart," replied the young knight. "I should like to see one of these wandering merchants. Perhaps he may have some new song to sing us."

The servant accordingly went to the door, and admitted a man so old that he was bent nearly double. His long white beard descended below his waist, and he seemed very feeble, and he hobbled up to the table.

"Good evening to you, gallants, and my fair ladies," he said, peering at the assembled company through a pair of horn-rimmed spectacles. "I have kept the pick of my budget for you—fine English needles, fine French lace, a snuff-box fair enough for a king to snuff from, a book of ballads—will you buy, my lord?" he said, approaching Sir James.

To please the old man a few purchases were made, and then Sir James asked whether he could not sing some country ballad.

After having drained a bumper of wine the pedlar complied.

"I will sing you," he said, "a new song called 'The Eagle and the Fox.'" And raising a crooked forefinger, he began in a quavering old voice to sing his simple ballad:—

A fox there was, as I've heard tell,
　Fol de rol derido,
Who did not love the eagle well,
　Fol de rol derido.
Said he, "The monarch of the air
He robs me of my daily fare;
But thraw his neck I do not dare,
　Tol de rol derido."

The fox he sought the weazel's aid,
　Fol de rol derido,
And to that cunning beast he said,
　Fol de rol derido,
"If you will rob the eagle's nest,
I'll freely treat you to the best,
So lend an ear to my behest,
　Tol de rol derido."

The weazel vowed he would not fail,
　Fol de rol derido,
But soon returned without his tail,
　Fol de rol derido.
The fox, he snarled, so I've heard tell;
The other said, "I ken full well
Ye dare not do the deed yoursel',
　Tol de rol derido."

"A pretty fable," said Sir Ralph; "but you shall interpret it, old man, for I vow there is some hidden meaning in it. Who is the fox and who is the eagle?"

"Nay, I know not," replied the pedlar, with a sly look. "I am but a simple body, and know naught of the affairs of my betters; though now I come to think on it, I have heard that the fox has a name not unknown in Scotland. Belike he stands in the song for some great nobleman."

If the laird had listened attentively to the song he might have thought that it was founded upon his own relations with Rob Roy and Moncrieff, but he was somnolent, and had not understood the drift of the song.

The pedlar now addressed him very earnestly :

"Laird," he said, "I have a jewel in my budget I will offer to no man but you, and I would fain see you alone."

The laird started up. He thought that perhaps the pedlar had had a motive for forcing his way into the hall, and was the bearer of some secret tidings.

For this reason he complied, with a jest to the company, with the old man's request, and led him into a small chamber near the outer door of the castle.

"Now, fellow," he said, "are we private enough ? Where is this fine jewel ? "

The pedlar, standing between him and the door, suddenly straightened himself, flung off his spectacles and his long, white beard, and there stood revealed to the eyes of the astonished laird his daring enemy, Rob Roy.

"MacLean of Glentive," said Rob Roy, "you have forbidden me to set foot in Glentive, and so I have come under your very roof-tree to show the scorn I bear ye for the scurvy tricks you have played me. But there my vengeance has an end. I am willing to bury the past, and, as a proof that my words are true, see, my dirk is sheathed. You are an unarmed man, and your life is in my hands this moment, here, in your own house, but I spare to strike you."

"You thieving rogue ! " cried the laird. "I have but to raise my voice and my servants will bind ye fast. Know, Rob Roy, that I have dungeons strong enough to hold even you."

"And know, Glentive," replied the chief, "that I have men enough to break the bars of the strongest prison ever built. Raise your voice and I will raise mine, and, though your varlets may slay me, my Highland laddies will avenge my fall, for they are not far away."

The laird was beside himself with passion. In another moment he would have alarmed the household, and Rob Roy in all likelihood might have been overpowered ; but at that moment Effie MacLean slipped softly into the room. Her feminine curiosity had been pro-

voked by the mention of the imaginary jewel, and truth compels us to admit that she had been standing outside the door, which was ajar.

She ran to her father, and put her white hand upon his mouth.

"You shall not cry out, father," she said ; "indeed you shall not. I hold it shame for two Christian gentlemen to live in such hatred of one another. And, indeed, it were unfair to call many to take one man."

MacLean put his daughter from him. "Go, child ! " he said, sternly ; "what follows anon will be no sight for your eyes ! "

Alarmed by this statement, which seemed intended as a hint that there would be bloodshed, Effie only grew more persistent in her intention of preserving peace.

"But I say Rob Roy shall depart in safety, as he came," said she.

"He has put foul scorn upon me ! " roared MacLean, "and I know how to recompense such insolence."

"Oh ! go, sir ! " said Effie, turning to the MacGregor,. "Go quickly ! The door is close at hand."

But Rob Roy stood, watching her.

"I am glad to have found so fair an advocate," he said. "Just now I was in a mood to cause some trouble in this house, but I will put that thought from me."

"Ay," she said, "and I trust you will live peaceably with my father in future."

"It was not I who began the strife," said Rob Roy, "and it is not I who wish to continue it."

"Father, will you not forget your quarrel with this gentleman ? " pleaded Effie.

But MacLean was sullen and silent.

At last he spoke.

"No," he said, "I forget nothing, this insolence of his least of all. Yet I would not have any brawling here to-night. He may go as he came. But the next time he comes hither it will be with the sword that I shall meet him."

Rob Roy smiled grimly. "I ask no more," he said. Then he turned to Effie. "I wonder you befriend that arch-rogue and outlaw, that thief Rob Roy," he said, "for you must have heard many an ill tale of him in these parts."

"I have heard that Rob Roy is good

to the poor and friendless," she replied, "that he is the brave champion of the oppressed. Good-night, sir, I pray you tarry no longer."

"Good-night, and joy be with you," said Rob Roy, gravely. Then, with a half-quizzical glance at the irate laird, he left the room and the castle.

MacLean went back to the banquetting hall, but his brow was so gloomy as he sat at table that his guests began to wonder if the strange old pedlar had brought him some evil tidings.

"I was a fool to let him go," thought MacLean, "though his detention would have meant an attack upon the castle. But I will humble the insolent MacGregor yet.

CHAPTER VI.

The Eagle's Nest.

MacLean's chagrin at the slight which had been put upon him by Rob Roy was so great that, at risk of seeming rude to his guests, he announced that business of urgent importance obliged him to be absent a few days in Edinburgh. Leaving the castle in charge of his sister, he set out, accompanied by only one servant. But it was not to Edinburgh that he went. When he reached the Duke of Montrose's domains he turned aside, and went to visit a certain Dugald Grahame, who was kin to the Duke, but who had fallen into disfavour with his noble kinsman.

This Dugald was a sour, crafty fellow, for whom the Laird of Glentive had no great liking at ordinary times; but in his present mood the laird was ready to fraternise with any man who could call Rob Roy his enemy.

Dugald Grahame, who lived in a building that was half-farmhouse, half fortress, received MacLean hospitably enough.

And when the two were alone together MacLean opened his heart to the dour Grahame.

"Aye ken, Dugald," he said, "I've lately been with the Duke in Edinburgh. Man, it's a pity you should let matters rest as they are betwixt you and your noble cousin, for a more gracious nobleman I never yet met."

"And how am I to regain his favour, Glentive?" said Dugald Grahame; "tell me that, and you will be making me your debtor."

"It's about that that I would speak to ye," said MacLean, eagerly. "There is a sure way to the Duke's heart."

"Show me the way, and you may be sure I'll take it," replied Dugald. who knew the advantage of standing well with those in high places.

The laird drew his chair nearer to Dugald's.

"Man, do ye ken what the Duke and I were plotting in Edinburgh? Ay, we put our heads together to hatch a plot, and if it came to naught it was because we had for our agent a man of no worth or character. If you would please the Duke you must make a prisoner of that noted robber and outlaw, Rob Roy."

"And if you would please my youngest wean you must give him the moon," returned Dugald, sarcastically.

"But I tell you it's not impossible," said the laird. "Who is Rob Roy that he should defy us, or be more difficult to take than another?"

"Ay, who indeed!" replied Dugald. "Rob Roy is cousin to the eagles, and you must climb in perilous places if you would harry the eagle's nest."

"I grant you the task is not easy, but why should we not accomplish it—you and I, Dugald, at the head of a dozen braw fighters?"

Dugald Grahame remained thoughtful for a minute. "Ay, it would please the Duke," he said.

"It would that."

"Do ye ken where Rob Roy is now? He is in his cave that he calls the Eagle's Nest."

"That is sure proof that he fears the Duke," said MacLean.

"It is proof that he is canny enough to keep his eyes open when his enemies are active."

"Well, we will harry the Eagle's Nest. I tell you plainly, Dugald, that my people have been sore harassed by the MacGregors of late, and I will have my revenge. But I will not march against Rob Roy as the Laird of Glentive, for that would bring the MacGregors into my glen again. It is in disguise I will go up to the Eagle's Nest, and I would counsel you to do the same. Then, whether we succeed or fail, we shall not draw upon our tenants the vengeance of the MacGregors. But we shall succeed."

With a little more persuasion Dugald

Grahame consented to act with MacLean. The attack upon Rob Roy was to be sudden and secret, and all the men taking part in it were to be garbed in plain kilts, so that the MacGregors could not hold any clan accountable for the capture of their chief.

Having made up his mind to act, Grahame lost no time in preparing for the projected attack, and the following day he and the laird, with ten picked men, left his house and marched out amongst the mountains.

The Eagle's Nest was two thousand feet up a mountain side, and could only be approached by a rocky path, which became, as it neared the cave, a narrow ledge with a precipitous slope on one side of it.

The attack was to be made by night, for there was more chance then of finding Rob Roy in the cave. A moonlight night had been chosen, for it would have been next to impossible to find the path in the dark.

Accordingly, in the white moonlight MacLean and the Grahames began their noiseless ascent of the mountain.

The climb was toilsome, until the ledge was reached, and here the progress of the warlike party became perilous. None but Highlanders or mountain sheep could have walked with any confidence along that rocky ledge, where a stumble might mean a swift glissade into the valley two thousand feet below.

But MacLean of Glentive, who led the way, advanced along this dangerous path steadily enough, holding his sheathed sword aside so that the scabbard should not clink against the rocky wall on his right hand. He beheld the yawning gulf on his left without any dizziness, and his heart was full of fierce resolution.

The man who had put him to scorn in his own house should be favoured with a return visit that would make him repent of his raids into Glentive.

With noiseless tread the fierce Highlanders followed MacLean, all eager to earn the Duke's blood-money, for Dugald had told them, truthfully enough, that Montrose would pay them royally if they succeeded in capturing or killing Rob Roy.

Clinging to the mountain-side they made their way along the winding ledge, until at last MacLean passed in front of them round a corner and halted. He had come into full view of the mouth of the cave.

He whispered this intelligence to Dugald, who was just behind him, and the news was passed back along the line.

With redoubled caution MacLean crept on. In front of the cave the path became a wide ledge, where a man might find room to draw his sword, and to swing it, too, if the MacGregors issued from the Eagle's Nest.

Inch by inch, scarcely breathing, MacLean moved nearer and nearer to the rocky platform. But he had not advanced far before a lump of rock gave way beneath his left foot. MacLean would have fallen had not Dugald thrust out his hand and saved him. But the rock went crashing and bounding into the valley far below, and, at the sound, a swart, silent figure appeared instantly in the mouth of the cave.

"Who comes?" cried this ready sentinel.

Then he clapped his musket to his shoulder and fired, seeing a man garbed in a kilt that told him not whether the tresspasser was friend or foe.

The bullet struck the rock above MacLean's head, and the laird withdrew behind the projecting corner.

"It's all over, man," said Dugald. "I kenned we should not catch the MacGregor napping."

"Then we'll catch him waking, Dugald," retorted the laird, valiantly "We have not climbed so high for nothing at all."

Though the laird spoke stoutly, he knew well enough that his situation was a desperate one. He must necessarily go first to the assault. Even if it had been possible for him to fall to the rear his pride would have prevented him. He had instigated this attack. There was nothing for it but to round the corner once more, and make a sudden dash towards the platform in front of the cave. But it seemed a thousand chances to one that a bullet would stop his progress before he was half-way to the cave. The sentinel, having recovered from his surprise, would not miss a second time.

In spite of the terrible odds against him, the laird, without a tremor, rounded the corner and came into view of the cave again.

To his astonishment the sentinel, instead of having been reinforced, had disappeared. Expecting every moment to see the flash of a musket issue from the cave, he went swiftly along the moonlit ledge and gained the broad platform. The wondering Grahames followed him; the whole attacking party found themselves peering into the cavern, from which proceeded not a sound.

"There's naebody here," said Dugald; "the eagle has flown."

"Then, by St. Andrew, we'll bide in his nest ourselves till he returns!" said MacLean.

One of the men had hastily kindled a torch he had found and lifted it over his head. The cave, which went thirty feet into the mountain side, was empty, except for several couches of dried fern that littered the floor.

"Where is the fellow that fired at me?" demanded MacLean.

"That's easily answered," replied Dugald; "the path goes on beyond the cave, and when ye popped back behind the rocks he just went on to warn his chief."

"Aweel! let the MacGregor come," retorted MacLean; "he'll find that we can hold his house against him. This is better than I looked for. So there was only one man in the cave!"

"And the chief may approach it by the way we have come," replied Dugald, "and so walk into our arms without warning."

The Grahames were highly delighted at the posture of affairs. They were in possession of Rob Roy's mountain eyrie, and there was some chance of his entering it unsuspectingly, when he could be easily made prisoner. But if he decided to leave them in temporary possession of it, they would, on quitting it, so break away the rocky path on either side of it, that this mountain fastness would never again be accessible to the bold chief of the MacGregors.

To destroy his favourite and safest hiding place would be to make some slight return for stolen cattle and for all the slights he had put upon them.

The twelve men, with their drawn claymores across their knees and loaded pistols beside them, sat silent upon the floor of the cavern. Now and again one of them would go to the mouth of the cave and look out. There was no sign of life outside, only the wide moonlit valley and the mountains, dim and misty, beyond it.

"I'm thinking we shall not catch him this time," said Dugald. "He will be off and away down Glentive while you sit here."

"Losh, man, he will not know it is I who am here," said MacLean. "But it may indeed be that he will not have the heart to make an attack upon this place, which he himself knows to be all but impregnable. And though it grieves me that he should have escaped my vengeance again, yet I am glad that we shall have the laugh of him, and he will never know who has done him the favour of cutting him off from the Eagle's Nest!"

The dawn grew grey, and the occupants of the cave were becoming drowsy. One by one they dropped off to sleep. MacLean had announced that he would keep watch. But the long climb had fatigued even him, and at last he sat down near the mouth of the cave and followed the example of his companions.

The laird of Glentive was wakened by a sound of choking. He started up, and immediately gasped for breath. His eyes smarted horribly as he strove in vain to see about him.

The cave was full of dense, acrid smoke; its occupants were all awake now, and all gasping for breath.

"'Tis the red thief who has done this," gasped MacLean. His angry ejaculations were cut short by a fit of coughing.

"Ye kept sair watch, MacLean!" cried Dugald, hidden in the smoke, and his utterance, too, was cut short.

Banked up against the mouth of the cave was a huge, smouldering bonfire. Scarcely a flame rose from it, for the fuel was damp. The wind blew the thick smoke straight into the cave.

"Push down the fire!" cried MacLean; and the men probed at it vainly with their claymores.

"Use your hands," gasped MacLean, himself setting the example.

A musket report just without the cave warned the prisoners that any interference with the bonfire would be recompensed with lead.

"Who's that that meddles with my fire?" cried a well-known voice outside. "May not I and my lads warm ourselves? The air is chill out here."

"You villain!" cried the choking laird, "we're smothered with the reek!"

"Aye, ye see the folly of harrying an eagle's nest," was the cool reply.

"Murderer! would you kill us all?"

"No, nor any one of you," replied Rob Roy.

" Pull down the fire."

" So I will when you have thrown out your arms." The choking prisoners could scarcely find breath to discuss terms. MacLean was speechless, but one man found breath enough to promise Rob Roy anything. A portion of the bonfire was pulled away, and a narrow aperture, through which daylight became visible, was made.

Through this swords and pistols were flung pell-mell, and then the smouldering fuel was quickly scattered, and the prisoners stepped out to inhale long draughts of the pure, morning air, and to find themselves face to face with Rob Roy and some half-dozen of his clansmen.

It was a bitter moment for the laird of Glentive. His enemy had got the better of him again, and he was unarmed, and at his mercy.

CHAPTER VII.

OPEN WAR.

There was a mischievous smile on Rob Roy's face.

" I tasted of your hospitality awhile back, Glentive," he said, " in your castle, and now you shall taste of mine."

The smoke had cleared out of the cave, and the men who had come to take Rob Roy prisoner were obliged to re-enter the cave as prisoners.

And here the outlawed chief gave them a substantial repast. Venison, oatmeal, a firkin of clear water, whisky and bread, were produced as if by magic from the rocky walls of the cave.

The disappointed Grahames were too hungry to refuse such good fare, but they ate in silence, and with gloomy brows. They knew not what Fate had in store for them. Rob Roy was no lover of bloodshed, but he was not likely to deal too leniently with men who had forced their way into his hiding-place with intent to destroy him.

It puzzled them to know how they had been trapped in the cave, but they supposed that the man whom MacLean had seen had gone to summon Rob Roy from a distance. As a matter of fact Rob Roy had been in the cave when they approached, but had left it, not by the mouth of the cave, but by moving a slab of stone at the inner end of it, and so entering a narrow, artificial passage, which wound round,

and opened on to the path beyond the cave. For the MacGregor was too wary to choose a hiding-place from which there was only one means of egress.

MacLean and his allies had to endure the taunts of the MacGregors with impotent wrath, and MacLean himself felt that nothing but the death of his enemy would satisfy him now. The triumphant way in which Rob Roy constantly eluded all efforts made to capture him was galling in the extreme ; so even while the laird was Rob Roy's prisoner he was devising fresh schemes of vengeance.

But these could not be put into execution now. Rob Roy gave orders for all to prepare to march. The captured arms were stored in the cave, and then the whole party left the Eagle's Nest.

Three armed MacGregors went first along the rocky ledge, and the unarmed prisoners followed, an inglorious procession. At the tail of them went Rob Roy, and three more of his men.

Thus escorted, the Grahames, in their nondescript garments, were marched down the mountain side, and away into the heart of the MacGregor's country, where their escort was strongly reinforced. All day long the wretched men were paraded among the villages, the object of derision to Rob Roy's clansmen, for their plan of going out to fight without their kilts and plaids of Grahame tartan provoked the contempt of all who saw them.

" They may well be ashamed of their tartan," said one observer.

" Cut off their ears," was a frequent cry.

" Put them in the river," suggested those more mercifully inclined.

But Rob Roy contented himself with dismissing all his prisoners before nightfall, with the exception of MacLean and Dugald Grahame.

Before dismissing the prisoners, however, Rob Roy fiercely warned them that if they visited the Eagle's Nest again they should feel the eagle's talons.

" And now, MacLean, and you, Dugald Grahame, I shall hold ye both to ransom," said Rob Roy.

" Indeed, you shall do no such thing," muttered MacLean to himself ; " you have taken hold of my cattle, but you shall have none of my gold. No, no, the laird of Glentive is not a man to buy his liberty so long as he has his two hands free."

In short, MacLean was determined to escape from custody, and to make another attempt to avenge all the indignities he had suffered at Rob Roy's hands.

The chance of escape did not occur that night, for the two captives were lodged in an upper room of a lofty house, belonging to one of Rob Roy's kinsmen.

Next day MacLean and Dugald Grahame were entrusted to the care of half-a-dozen MacGregors, to whom Rob Roy gave instructions to conduct them to one of the islands on Loch Lomond. Then Rob Roy himself took ironical leave of MacLean.

The laird of Glentive and his companion in misfortune were then hurried along, much to their indignation, towards Loch Lomond. MacLean's anger grew greater with every step he took, and his wounded pride prompted him to devise all manner of imaginary acts of revenge upon Rob Roy.

With long strides the little band hurried through the heather, coming at last to the very outskirts of MacLean's own country, and here the eagle-eyed MacGregors kept a sharp watch.

It was just after their midday halt when, on turning a corner, MacLean's heart leaped with joy, for immediately in front of them was a large body of his own men returning from some distant market.

The MacLeans recognised the laird at once, saw the posture of affairs, and, with wild cries, rushed forward to rescue him.

In vain the MacGregors tried to carry off their prisoners. They made a gallant stand, but six claymores were of no avail against four times that number. Perhaps if Rob Roy himself had been with them the matter might have turned out differently; as it was the Mac-Gregors drew off in good order and the MacLeans did not pursue them, but gathered round the laird.

"Send word through the clan," he said, "let every man who can come meet me to-night by the Headless Cross, for by St. Andrew, I will not return home until that insolent thief, Rob Roy, is either dead or in safe keeping in Stirling Castle."

When the setting sun reddened the slopes of heather that evening, MacLean, arrayed now in the tartan of his clan, for which he had sent a messenger home to Glentive Castle, stood beside the Headless Cross, a great granite monument of unknown origin, and saw the red light glint on a hundred claymores.

Every claymore was grasped by the hand of a stalwart MacLean, and fierce were the shouts that greeted the laird's invitation to them to follow him against the men who had so often despoiled them of their cattle.

The laird was fully roused now. He had tried to take Rob Roy by artifice, keeping his own share in the business dark, now he meant open war.

In close order the MacLeans set out to invade the MacGregors' country, with their plaids about them, and their claymores swinging by their sides. Some of them carried muskets or pistols.

MacLean knew where to find Rob Roy; he had heard that morning that he intended to visit a kinsman of his who dwelt in a lonely farm at the foot of a beetling cliff, not many miles from the Eagle's Nest, and thither he led his men.

The MacLeans reached the farm at sunrise. The laird smiled a grim smile when he saw the humble farm-house. Such a small place could make no defence against a dozen men, still less against a hundred. His only fear was that the bird might be flown.

"Make no sound till I give the word," he commanded; and the hundred men advanced in silence up one side of the ridge of ground which still lay between them and the farm. The laird's intention was that his men should halt a moment on the top of the ridge, and then, raising their war cry, rush down upon the farm in a manner calculated to strike dismay into the heart of any MacGregor that ever breathed. Rob Roy would then, he thought, surrender without parley—indeed, he would not be given the chance of parley.

This imposing advance, however, was not to take place. When the MacLeans reached the top of the ridge they saw that a river flowed in front of the house. The wild rush upon the place which had been contemplated was impossible.

"Curse the red fox," said the laird, stamping his foot with mortification. "I might have known that he would not bide anywhere but where all the approaches were safeguarded. Forward, MacLeans; the clan have wetted their feet in the blood of their foes ere now, and shall they be daunted by water?"

In his impetuosity the laird ran out in front of his men, dashed down the slope, and stepped boldly into seven feet of water.

The laird of Glentive was a man of many accomplishments, but, alas, he could not swim! Over his angry red face, over his gay plumed bonnet swirled the deep water, and he was only saved by Duncan, his free-spoken factor, who had tramped dolorously beside him through the night, and who now flung him the end of his plaid, and drew him to the bank.

The laird scrambled out, raging and spluttering.

"Eh, laird, laird," said Duncan, "curb your wrath, man. Had it been whisky and water maybe we would have followed you intil the stream; but, ye ken, we're no fushes."

The laird's anger was not softened by the sound of a loud laugh.

Rob Roy had come to the gate of the farmhouse, and had witnessed the laird's discomfiture.

"What, Glentive," he shouted, "ye're in a sair hurry to bring me your ransom."

"MacLean of Glentive has no need to buy his liberty," shouted the laird, "but I've brought my ransom, Rob Roy—a hundred braw laddies with claymores."

"Ay," replied Rob Roy, "a hundred braw laddies that canna cross a puddle of water!"

The laird looked up and down the stream, but there was no bridge in sight. Some of the men were ready to plunge in and swim, but the laird would suffer no man to cross before himself, for he wished to cut down Rob Roy with his own hand.

He sent his men scouring in all directions for fallen trees, chafing meanwhile at the delay which would give Rob Roy a chance, if he cared to take it, of escape.

But the chief stood at the gate of the house, with a look of careless amusement on his face. When he calmly took a pinch of snuff it was too much for the laird, who snatched a musket from a bystander, and fired at the chief.

The bullet broke a pane of glass.

"Eh! MacLean, man, you should curb your anger," said Rob Roy, with a solemn shake of the head. Then he retired slowly into the house, and soon appeared at the broken window with a sword in his hand.

In the meantime the MacLeans had found two fallen fir trees, tall enough to span the stream. They flung these across side by side, and began the passage of the river. So eager were they to get over that many of them did not wait their turn at this improvised bridge, but plunged into the water and clung to the ends of plaids held out to them by comrades on the bridge, so that many men stepped across the bridge with their plaids trailing at either end in the water and a man clinging to either end.

Thus, in a few minutes the MacLeans were all mustered on the further side of the river, and then, with the laird in front, rushed forward and surrounded the house.

The laird himself dashed at the door. It was of solid oak, studded with iron nails, and strongly set in a porch of massive masonry. All the lower windows of the house were barred. The unpretending farmhouse was a fortress of no mean strength.

"Have you hurt your knuckles by rapping at the door, Glentive?" cried a mocking voice from one of the upper windows.

"Fire at the windows!" roared the laird to his men, and there was the crash of musketry and of broken glass.

"We have him now, safe enough," said the laird, exultantly. "He's as safe as if already lodged in gaol."

But although the house was surrounded and Rob Roy's escape seemed impossible, it was equally impossible to get at him through the door or the lower windows.

"Come down, man, come down and surrender to save needless bloodshed!" cried the laird, standing in front of the house in view of the upper windows.

The occupants of the farmhouse, who numbered only two men beside Rob Roy, had arms in abundance, but unfortunately—or perhaps fortunately—were entirely without powder. The laird, of course, did not know this, so in standing so close to the house exhibited a boldness which won Rob Roy's generous admiration. Even if he had had a charge in his pistol he would have spared the laird, for he had not forgotten the laird's daughter, and had no wish to make her an orphan; but he intended to further incense the bellicose laird who treated him with such vindictive spite, nevertheless.

Finding that Rob Roy would not listen to " reason " the laird ordered his men to enter the house through the upper windows, which were three in number. He himself intended to enter by the window at which Rob Roy had been seen.

Two tall clansmen stood beneath this window, another leapt on to their shoulders, and the laird ascended this living ladder and clutched at the sill of the window.

Instantly there was a flicker of steel, and the plume of the laird's bonnet was shorn away. As, however, this did not daunt him, Rob Roy struck him smartly over his head with the flat of his sword. The laird toppled over and fell, bruised and furious, on the turf beneath. At the other windows his clansmen had fared no better. One of them had, indeed, been rather badly wounded in the shoulder.

" MacLeans! " roared the laird. " Will you be shamed like this? There are but three of them, as I think, and shall it be said that three MacGregors defied a hundred MacLeans? "

The fierce Highlanders again swarmed up living ladders to the upper windows, but were pushed down, one after another, until bruises and even broken bones were plentiful.

Then several of them set to work to try and wrench away the bars of the lower windows; but these were too stout and too firmly fixed to yield, and by-and-by the defenders of the house met these attackers with cascades of hot water, which discouraged them not a little.

" Fetch the tree trunks! " shouted the laird. " We'll have the door down. They have no fire-arms or they would have used them ere now, so you may do your work in safety."

In a few minutes a dozen men dashed at the door with the butt end of one of the fallen firs. The door might have been made of solid granite for all the effect this had upon it. Again and again with a heavy thud the tree struck the door, and still the door held fast.

" Glentive! " cried Rob Roy, at last. ' I would speak with ye."

" Ah! he sees the uselessness of re-sistance at last," ejaculated the laird to Duncan.

" Maybe ay, and maybe no," said Duncan, " but give an ear to what he has to say. It will allow these poor lads time to wipe the sweat from their faces."

" Speak on," said the laird.

" I must have your promise that your men will not shoot me if I come to the window," said Rob Roy.

" No, no; they shall not shoot," said the laird. " I would liefer take you alive than dead, Rob Roy, and let the law do its own work upon you."

Thus reassured Rob Roy leaned out of a window. " MacLean," he said, " let me tell you you do but waste your time. Look at your men, nursing their broken limbs, MacLean. Why expose the poor fellows to further perils, Glentive? Ye'll not catch me, my mannie; go home, go home, and take a turn at the spinning-wheel. I bear you no ill-will, though you have hatched one or two ugly plots against me. And know that I'm as safe here as the King is in London."

Rob Roy withdrew. This speech ren-dered the laird speechless with rage, for if the MacGregor designed to spare his life he did not mean to spare his feel-ings.

" The proud fool needs a lesson," said Rob Roy to one of the MacGregors who was with him in the house. " I thought the man was my friend till lately, and I do not wish to harm him, but he shall see that he does but make himself ridi-culous when he meddles with me."

The MacGregors then retired from the windows.

Meanwhile MacLean had drawn off his men, in a wide circle about the house. It was true that many of them were wounded, and the laird wished to spare them any further wounds.

" It is for me to settle with the red thief," he said, " and for me alone, with my own sword. If he will not come down and fight me of his own accord, we must make him come."

Advancing again to within speaking distance, Maclean cried out:

" Rob Roy, I challenge you to come down and fight me, man to man, and not one of my men shall stir a finger."

" No, no, laird," said Rob Roy, " we've played that game before, and I sent your bonny bit claymore twirling in the air. If I fight you again I shall cut off your head. You're no match for me, MacLean; I will not fight with a bairn."

" Madman, dare ye brave me thus ! " shouted **MacLean.** " I'll make you come down to me."

He then retired and ordered his men to draw their circle a little closer about the house, so as to set about a dozen men free without lessening the space between man and man. The dozen were then sent to collect as many dried pine branches as they could gather.

They returned quickly with armfuls. A bonfire was kindled near the house with these, and the burning brands were snatched from it by MacLean and the dozen men told off for this duty.

They ran towards the house, expecting every moment to be fired upon, and flung the burning branches through the broken windows of the upper storey, and thrust them through the barred windows of the ground floor.

" Hearken, you red thief," shouted the laird, " you fought us with smoke, and I'll fight you with fire. Now will you come out and fight me ? "

" You're a hard man, MacLean," cried the voice of Rob Roy from within.

" Surrender, then," replied the laird with delight, for he thought the bold MacGregor was at last convinced that resistance was useless.

" Oh, the reek ! the reek ! " cried Rob Roy ; " it will smother me ! "

" Come down, Rob Roy, come down and surrender," persisted the laird.

" My lads will take toll of your cattle for this morn's work," answered Rob Roy.

" The insolent thief defies us still. Bring more fire ! " roared the laird.

A dozen nimble fellows ran to the bonfire and returned with more flaming branches. In all the windows they thrust or threw them. The interior of the house was fairly in a blaze at last.

" Go back," said the laird to the men who had helped him to fire the house, " and let the circle be drawn closer so that none can break through it."

The men obeyed. The flames crackled and roared in the house, and the laird, with drawn sword, awaited his enemy in front of the porch.

The MacLeans, stern and silent, stood all round the house, wondering.

They thought that Rob Roy had chosen to perish in the flames, and were a little awed, perhaps, to think that this was the end of a man whose name was now a household word in Scotland, whose deeds, wild or generous, were on every tongue.

The flames shot in lurid tongues from the windows, and the laird had to edge further and further away from the house ; but he still kept watch, sword in hand.

" He is waiting in some room where the flames have not yet reached," he thought, " and thinks to make a dash for it when we believe him to be dead."

" Draw closer, men, draw closer," he cried to his followers, determined there should be no way of escape through that circle of kilted men. Then he shouted, " Rob Roy, are ye afraid to measure swords with me ? " Even the laird could have wished a better end for a brave man, bitter enemy though he was.

The flames roared on, the sparks streaming up in the morning air.

At last the roof fell in with a crash.

" Come away, laird, come away ! " growled Duncan, twitching at the laird's sleeve. " You've had your revenge at last, and it's a proud man ye ought to be ! "

The laird looked angrily at his factor, not liking the tone of reproach in his voice.

" He might have died by the sword of a MacLean," he said, as if he deemed this a high honour for anybody.

At that moment a shrill call, clear and cheery, came through the air. It was the war-cry of the MacGregors.

Glentive raised his eyes. On the beetling cliff beyond the ruined house, midway up on a dizzy ledge, stood Rob Roy, waving his bonnet to the astonished MacLeans. He had a man on either side of him, and the three MacGregors woke the echoes of the valley with their derisive yells.

" Yon's a brave man," said the factor.

The laird said nothing at all. Rob Roy was plainly invincible. An underground passage had led him away from the burning house, under the very feet of the MacLeans who were waiting to take him.

Within twenty-four hours the MacGregors had again raided Glentive, driving away more cattle than would compensate them for the burnt farm house.

And MacLean of Glentive returned his castle and his guests moody, dispirited but still resolved upon revenge.

CHAPTER VIII.

A TREACHEROUS KNIGHT.

" I wish to speak to you, Sir Ralph, on a very private matter," said Sir James Oldcastle to his fellow guest at Glentive Castle, when the two young men were pacing a walk in the castle garden, one evening towards sunset.

"We both love the laird's daughter, Ralph, and there's the truth of it ; and it is as plain as a pikestaff that we cannot both marry her."

" That is very true," replied Sir Ralph, after a pause.

" Now," said Sir James, " I should be sorry if there were any ill-blood between us over this, so I suggest that we make a compact, here and now, that the loser agrees to stand by the winner. Whichever of us is so fortunate as to win the lady's hand shall have the loyal support of the other. Do you agree ? I have a reason for proposing this."

" I agree," replied Sir Ralph; " it is a fair enough compact. But what is your reason for it ? "

" My reason is, Ralph, that the winner will need a friend to help him outface the wrath of the laird."

" Do you say so ? "

" Ay, I do, indeed. The laird is a kindly host, but a very choleric man, and a Highlander into the bargain, with more than his share of Highland pride. I have been sounding his factor, Duncan MacLean, a very sly, shrewd old body, and he told me that the laird has sworn a hundred times that his daughter shall, marry none but a Highlander. His scorn of Lowlanders you know. Englishmen he will bear with, but he will not willingly give his daughter to an Englishman, for, says Duncan, he has no respect for our English fashion of reckoning our wealth in money. The Highlander, you know, reckons his wealth in men."

" Say you so, indeed ? " said Sir Ralph. " I thought the laird had some regard for money."

" He has more for feudal power and long descent, and the pedigree must be a Scotch one, or he will not regard it at all."

" You surprise me. But I agree to your proposal, Sir James. If you win, I stand by you. If I win, you stand by me."

" You swear it ? "

" I swear it."

The two young men clasped hands in the garden walk and then returned to the castle. Sir Ralph's heart was heavy ; he had been so engrossed in his own passion, in his own dreams of happiness, that he had not at first noticed Sir James's infatuation ; when he did observe it he tried to persuade himself that he was mistaken. But there was no longer room for doubt.

Sir Ralph had a very modest estimate of his own worth, and he felt assured in his own mind that Effie MacLean, if she favoured either suitor, would favour the dark and masterful knight, Sir James Oldcastle.

Only three days after this compact had been made, Sir James came into the apartments his friend occupied in the castle, his eyes aglow with excitement.

" You must wish me joy," he said, " and say you bear me no ill-will, for I shall take a bride home with me to Northumberland."

Poor Sir Ralph could not utter a word at first, so painful were the emotions that possessed him. However, he managed to stammer out some words of congratulation at last.

" And now," said Sir James, " I hope you remember our compact, for I shall have great need of your help."

" How ? Have you spoken to Mac-Lean on this subject ? "

" I have, and never before did I believe men could actually breathe fire."

" He was angry ? "

" Angry ! I thought he would eat me alive. He said the thing was not to be thought of, when he grew cooler ; my merits might be great for an Englishman, but his daughter should wed no one who had not the blood of Scottish kings in his veins. As for my wealth ! thank heaven, said he, he was no bailie-body, no Lowland huckster, ready to sell his daughter to the highest bidder."

" And so you have quarrelled ? "

" Ay, and made it up again, after a fashion. You will notice no change in his manner towards me. In his opinion the matter is at an end, so he has no more cause to be angry with me. MacLean of Glentive has spoken, and what he says is law."

" And what do you intend ? "

" Intend ? Why, my dear sir, to

ensure the lady's happiness, and my own. She has so great a dread of being forcibly married to some sandy-haired chieftain of her father's choosing that she is ready to elope with me to-morrow. And that is why I ask you to hold to your bargain. I want your help."

"I have promised it," faltered Sir Ralph.

"And so, my dear friend, I know you will give it, as loyally as I would have given you help, if you had stood in my shoes. There may be sword-work for us over this business, for the laird will pursue us, unless we are very wary."

Sir Ralph Couldrey, having given his promise to help his fortunate rival, now entered into his plans loyally.

"To leave the castle by stealth," said Sir James, "might prove fatal. Where the laird has so many retainers detection would be almost certain. So I intend that we shall set out openly in broad daylight. You look surprised. But what could be more easy? You, and I, and Miss MacLean set sail to-morrow afternoon for an outing on the loch. If the wind holds good two or three hours will take us many miles away from Glentive. We shall land far enough away to baffle pursuit, and procure horses to carry us south. Before we cross the Border Miss MacLean will become my Lady Oldcastle, since the marriage knot is easily tied in this country. But if there should be pursuit—well, two pairs of eyes are better than one, two swords are better than one. What say you?"

"I have given you my promise, and I will not break it."

"Ha! I knew it. And one thing more, Ralph. Do not speak to Miss MacLean of our projected marriage, unless she herself opens the subject. A maiden is shy about these matters."

"I understand," said poor Sir Ralph.

The following afternoon a small sailing boat put out on the wide loch. In it were the two Englishmen and Effie.

No mention was made by any of them of the purpose of their journey.

The boat crossed the loch, and Glentive Castle was now a mere speck in the distance.

Sir James suggested that they should land and inspect the ruins of an ancient abbey which stood near the water. When they were among the ruins Sir James took his friend aside, and said, "Go now, and push off the boat from the shore, and let it drift. We shall be pursued, and if the boat lies where it now is it will show where we landed."

With a heavy heart Sir Ralph returned to the beach, and sent the boat adrift. It was hard to see Effie Mac-Lean so happy with another man, for she had seemed very happy in the boat, and when wandering in the abbey ruins.

But when Sir Ralph returned to the abbey he found that her mood had changed indeed. She was standing face to face with Sir James Oldcastle, proud, angry, with flaming cheeks and flashing eye, and as Sir Ralph rejoined them she turned upon him.

"So, sir," she said, scornfully, "you requite my father's hospitality by plotting against my happiness and his. You would aid your friend to carry me off to England, would you? And is it not a gallant deed, for two gentlemen to trick a maiden thus? But I do not fear you. It is you who have most cause to fear, for there is not a man of the name of MacLean but will gird on his sword to pursue you, unless you take me back instantly to Glentive!"

"I plot against you!" exclaimed the astonished Sir Ralph. "Why, am I not furthering your wishes? Have you not promised to marry Sir James Oldcastle, against your father's wishes? He told me so."

"He told you! Ay, you may tell me that, but I do not believe you, Sir Dastard."

"Lady," said Sir Ralph, "when you call me that you wrong we as well as hurt me. I have spoken the truth." Then he turned upon Sir James.

"What means this?" he said, sharply.

"It means," said Sir James, with an uneasy smile, "that my lady has a fit of the tantrums. In this country it is the common fashion for a man to carry off his bride by force, and for the bride to feign reluctance. We are but following the fashion of the country. I assure you, Sir Ralph that I had this lady's consent to marry me, and to elope with me thus."

"Oh, shameful!" cried Effie. "You are well matched for friends, Sir Liar and Sir Dastard. I refused plainly to marry you, and well you know I meant it, and mean it. Take me back to Glentive; I command it."

"I will know the truth of this," said

Sir Ralph. Oldcastle turned to Effie. "Your lightest wish shall ever be law to me," he said, "when once we are married. With your present request I cannot comply. I cannot take you back to Glentive, for, see, my friend has sent the boat adrift. To go round the loch on foot would mean a three days' journey."

Effie MacLean gave a gasp of despair, and turned a look of horror and contempt upon Sir Ralph.

"Coward!" she said.

"I have been tricked," said Sir Ralph, "and I will see you righted. I turned the boat adrift to baffle pursuit, because I thought I should be serving you. But have no fear. You shall be safe. As for you, Sir James, you are a villain to play this trick upon us."

Sir James laughed. "By St. George," he said, "I am a man that likes to have his own way, and I mean to have my own way, and you are bound by oath to help me."

"I bound myself to help you if you won this lady's heart. It is clear that you are not so fortunate, and I will protect her from you with my sword."

CHAPTER IX.

The End of a Feud.

Sir Ralph marvelled that his friend should have thought that he would aid him in his villainous scheme.

As a matter of fact Sir James did not need Sir Ralph's help any longer and did not fear his enmity. His presence in the boat had been necessary, for Sir James could not have sailed it single-handed, and feared to employ any of MacLean's men. Sir Ralph Couldrey was, in the dark-browed knight's estimation, a mere stripling, who could not hinder his plans if he would not further them. His presence was, therefore, no inconvenience.

But Sir Ralph had more resolution than the other knew of. He drew his sword and said, "This shall ensure your good behaviour."

Sir James laughed.

"Put it by," he said, "and let us bandy no more words. One thing is certain, we cannot return to Glentive to-night, and, as the dews are falling, we had best press on until we reach some place of shelter, where we may be able to come to a happier understanding all round. I am resolved to take a bride home with me to Northumberland, and would fain do so without bloodshed."

"I shall not leave the shore," said Effie, defiantly, "for there may be fishermen putting out on the water who will pass within hail, and then, perhaps, I shall see justice done upon cowards."

Her persistence in regarding Sir Ralph as an enemy provoked the young man into a determination to prove to her his friendship.

Sir James caught Effie by the arm, not roughly, but with intent to hurry her away from the abbey ruins.

Upon this Sir Ralph at last raised his sword to strike him.

This moved Sir James Oldcastle to anger, and he loosed his hold on Effie.

"Very well," he said, "since you will have it so."

He wrenched his sword from its sheath, and the blades met with a clash. Effie MacLean, now aware that Sir Ralph was really her friend, as he had professed, stood with clasped hands, watching the deadly combat, and breathing silent prayers for the success of her champion.

The angry clatter of swords filled the air for some minutes, and then, with a groan, Sir Ralph threw up his arms and fell. Sir James stood panting beside him.

"There, madam," he said, to Effie, "see what your obstinacy has done. Had you accepted the inevitable at first this would not have happened."

Without heeding his words, Effie knelt by the wounded man, and staunched his wound.

Then she turned to Sir James. "Fetch some water," she said.

He obeyed her without a word. Quickly she did all she could to make the injured man easy. Then she rose, pale and defiant, and turned upon Oldcastle.

"Will this cure you of your madness?" she said. "Unless you mean to murder your friend you will do all you may to get him safely housed and tended. Go, get help. I will stay here."

"Miss MacLean," replied Sir James, firmly, "neither what has happened, nor anything that can happen, shall ever turn me from my purpose. I will make this man, who was foolish enough to resist me, as comfortable as may be in yon chantrey, which has still, as I see, a roof to it to keep off the rain. After that I shall take you away with me, and will send back hither those who shall take care of Sir Ralph, for I would not have him die. But you shall go on to England with me."

"Never!" cried Effie, vehemently; but the dark young man only smiled.

He made a couch of fern for his injured companion, under shelter of a broken roof, and then carried him to it.

In the meanwhile Effie MacLean had been looking about among the ruins for some hiding-place.

She spied, at length, a tower that had not crumbled away like the masonry that adjoined it.

There was a narrow doorway at the base of it, and through this she passed. The winding spiral stairway within was still intact. Hastily she went up the stairs, and got out upon the summit of the tower, whence she could see the broad, moonlit loch, which she scanned eagerly, but there were no boats upon it.

Sir James, having accomplished his work, began to look about for her, and she heard his harsh laugh when he first suspected she was hiding.

"He must not see me here," she thought, preparing to descend the stairs a little way.

But the moonlight was bright, and Sir James chanced to glance up at the tower and saw her.

"You have chosen a lofty nesting-place, my turtle-dove," he cried; "but I must take the liberty of leading you down again from there, for we must go on our way."

And he hastened towards the tower.

"Stay!" she cried, at last roused to desperation, "I forbid you to enter the tower. Will you leave your friend to bleed to death?"

"No," replied Sir James, "he is doing well enough, for the present, and I will send help to him; but you will come with me to summon help."

"I will not."

"You will, my lady." Again the knight laughed harshly, and drew nearer to the tower.

Then Effie leaned over the broken battlements.

"Sir James Oldcastle," she cried, in a clear, passionate voice, "as surely as you set foot upon the first step of the stairway I will fling myself down from here."

Still he only laughed, as he looked up, and saw her beautiful pale face with the moonlight upon it. Its beauty only made him the more anxious to reach her side. He did not wish to lose time by delay amongst these ruins, for pursuit was inevitable.

"Would you murder me too in your madness?" she said. "I tell you solemnly that if you climb to where I now stand it will be only to look down upon my lifeless body. Beware how you meddle with a MacLean."

"Ah, you would not be so cruel," replied Oldcastle. He stood on the threshold of the tower now. Effie saw him stoop to pass through the door.

Rising on the battlements she cried out, "God forgive me, it is the only way!"

In another instant she would have carried out her threat and gone headlong to her death; but at that moment a sepulchral voice cried "Stay!"

Her attention arrested, she looked down, and saw a figure, in Highland array, standing in a patch of moonlight, with one hand outstretched towards Sir James Oldcastle.

The latter turned, and advanced a little way towards this figure.

"Who are you?" he asked in an awed voice. The motionless figure, that seemed suddenly to have sprung from the ground, still stood with hand outstretched.

Effie MacLean fully believed it to be a spectre, the wraith of one of the nameless dead that had been buried long ago in the ancient burial-ground below.

"Who are you?" repeated Sir James, growing bolder.

"You have spilt blood upon my grave," replied the apparition. "You have violated the sanctity of this place. Beware, young man, for therefore must you die."

Sir James was not free from superstition. The place and the hour combined to heighten his fears. But, ghost or man, he would defend himself against this stranger with his sword. Not for all the ghosts in Scotland would he turn from his purpose.

He drew his sword once more.

"Have at you!" he cried, running forward.

The apparition also drew a sword, and advanced to meet the knight. Effie watched, spellbound. Her champion seemed to be a man, after all, a tall, sturdily-built man; at all events his sword was no ghostly weapon, but forged of good steel.

After the first clash of weapons Sir James drew back.

"What! is it not Rob Roy?" he said. "Now may you help me to a fine revenge upon your enemy, MacLean of Glentive!"

"Fool and coward!" cried Rob Roy, fiercely, "do you think the MacGregor wars on women? You merit death!"

Again their swords met, and after a fierce encounter the Englishman fell.

Sir James strove to rise, but sank back again and lay still. Then the victor looked up at Effie.

"Daughter of MacLean," he said, "you have seen that those who meddle with a MacLean have to reckon with Rob Roy. I ask you to come down to me, but not over the battlements."

With a cry of joy Effie descended the staircase and was greeted outside the tower by her father's enemy.

Rob Roy, returning from a lonely expedition to the shores of the loch, had seen the girl standing on the tower, and, drawing near, had recognised her and heard her conversation with Oldcastle.

After thanking the chief fervently for his timely aid, Effie glanced towards Old-castle.

"Is he dead?" she asked.

"No, he does not deserve to die by the sword of a chief," was the reply. "Your father shall do justice upon him."

Rob Roy then left her and returned an hour later by water with a fisherman.

The two wounded men were carried into the boat, and the whole party were soon sailing back to Glentive Castle.

It was nearly noon next day before the boat neared the castle quay. Long before the shore was reached the occupants of the boat had seen beach and quay thronged with people. MacLean himself towered above everyone at the quay head.

As the boat drew near Rob Roy could see the laird's broad face red with rage.

"You shall answer to me for this with your sword!" shouted MacLean. "This day shall end our quarrels, for one of us

two must fall. So it was you who detained my daughter; and what have you done to my guests?"

"They are both here!" cried Rob Roy, as the boat drew up against the quay.

A cry of horror went up from those on the quay as the laird's English guests were seen lying in the bottom of the boat swathed with blood-stained bandages.

"Infamous man," said MacLean, "do you bring the murdered bodies of my guests back to me, then? I swore that the next time you visited Glentive you should come hither to your doom, and now your fate is sealed."

"You will hear me first, father," said Effie, standing up with one hand against the mast of the boat. "I shall tell you how Sir Ralph Couldrey sought to save me and how Rob Roy did save me from a villain. Rob Roy, let me tell you, has shown himself to be the truest friend you have!"

A few minutes later Effie was telling her father the story of Oldcastle's perfidy.

At the conclusion of it the laird turned to his former foeman, who had just stepped out of the boat, and held out his hands to him.

"You have often wronged me, Glentive," said Rob Roy. "Say, have I wronged you now?"

"No, no, MacGregor. You have shown a noble generosity. Give me your hand. There can be no more bitterness between us."

And the two men clasped hands and the long feud was at an end.

There was a wedding at Glentive Castle a few weeks later, when Sir Ralph Couldrey wedded the laird's daughter. Sir James Oldcastle was not present on this occasion, although he was still at Glentive and recovered from his wound. For he was solitary in one of the castle dungeons, from which he was not suffered to depart until some weeks later. But prominent among the guests at the wedding was Rob Roy, the outlawed chief, who from that time forward reckoned the laird of Glentive among his warmest friends.

THE END.